For Linsay ~ or....

♡ x.

WHO KILLED AMANDA PALMER

This is the first edition of WHO KILLED AMANDA PALMER
self-published and limited to 10,000 copies.

THE RECORD ALBUM IS AVAILABLE FOR DOWNLOAD, ON CD AND ON VINYL.
YOU SHOULD BUY IT.

FOR THE SITE THAT CONTAINS EVERYTHING ABOUT THIS RECORD, INCLUDING STORIES ABOUT THE SONGS, THE PIANO/GUITAR SHEET MUSIC, ALL THE MUSIC VIDEOS, AND LOTS OF OTHER INTERESTING STUFF THAT YOU CAN'T FIND ANYWHERE ELSE, GO TO **WHOKILLEDAMANDAPALMER.COM**.

FOR INFORMATION ABOUT THE COLLECTED SONGS, PROJECTS AND JOURNAL OF AMANDA PALMER, PLEASE VISIT **AMANDAPALMER.NET**

WHO KILLED AMANDA PALMER

A COLLECTION OF PHOTOGRAPHIC EVIDENCE

WITH STORIES BY

NEIL GAIMAN

First published in the United States of America in 2009
by Eight Foot Books
c/o PS Business Management Inc.
140 West 57th Street
New York, NY 10019
www.whokilledamandapalmer.com

Lyrics: Amanda Palmer
Stories: Neil Gaiman
Cover Photograph: Gregory Nomoora
Art Directon: Beth Hommel and Amanda Palmer
Book Design: Beth Hommel, Harry Choron and Sandra Choron
Printed in China through InterPress Ltd.

Cataloging-in-Publication Data

Palmer, Amanda, 1976-
Who killed Amanda Palmer / by Amanda Palmer ; text,
Neil Gaiman ; photographs by Kyle Cassidy, Beth Hommel and others.
 p. cm.
LCCN: 2008941265
ISBN-13: 978-0-615-23439-7
ISBN-10: 0-615-23439-9

    1. Palmer, Amanda,--1976---Fiction. 2. Rock
musicians--United States--Fiction. 3. Rock musicians--
Death--Fiction. 4. Rock musicians--United States--
Pictorial works. 5. Rock music--2001-2010--Texts.
I. Gaiman, Neil. II. Cassidy, Kyle III. Title.
PS3616.A33882W46 2009   813'.6
QBI08-700249

EIGHT
FOOT

BOOKS

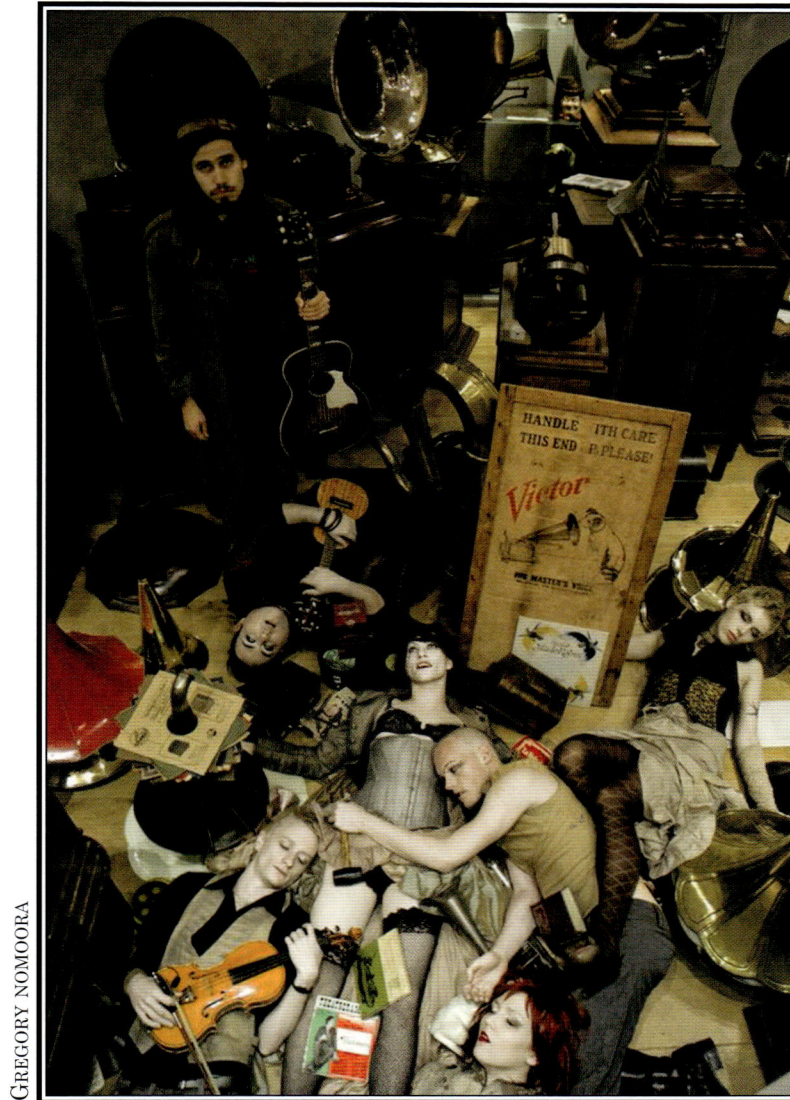

GREGORY NOMOORA

FOR JASON WEBLEY, THE ANSWER TO EVERYTHING

Yale University

SCHOOL OF ART

1156 Chapel St

december 19, 2008.   9:10 PM.

WHO KILLED AMANDA PALMER

A COLLECTION OF PHOTOGRAPHIC EVIDENCE

WITH STORIES BY NEIL GAIMAN

MUSIC AND LYRICS BY AMANDA PALMER

PHOTOGRAPHS BY KYLE CASSIDY, BETH HOMMEL and many others

Like you, I know exactly where I was and what I was doing when I heard Amanda Palmer had been killed.

Like you, I know no more than that. Killed, yes. But by whom and how none of us ever knew. There was nothing ever said about it on the television or the radio. But we knew, we knew.

Rumours multiplied. I met a Hell's Angel in a bar in Encino who swore blind that he knew a man who claimed to have crushed in Amanda's skull with lead piping, on behalf of a crazed ex-boyfriend.

It became a national obsession. "Who killed Amanda Palmer?" bubblegum cards were traded and traded again in schoolyards across America. I still own two of them: one shows Amanda's bullet-riddled corpse dangling from a wall; the other shows her body washed up on the shore of an unidentified lake, her face blue and puffy from the water, the claws of some crustacean pushing out from between her purple lips.

I remember the candlelight vigils, and the shrines, dozens of them, in cities all over the world, spontaneous demonstrations from people who no longer had an Amanda Palmer. They lit candles and left behind telephones, scalpels, exotic items of underwear, plastic figurines, children's picture books, antlers, love.

"She went as she would have wanted to go." That was what an Amanda Palmer impersonator told me in a pub off Carnaby Street. Much later that night, voice slurred by alcohol, the man confided in me that he was certain that the real Amanda Palmer had been "abducted by beings from a higher vibrational plane," and that the pictures of Amanda's death were not fakes, pasted-up and air-brushed in some back-alley photographic studio, but actual photographs of the deaths of "sister-selves," creatures grown from Amanda Palmer's own protoplasm.

Very young children made up songs about the different ways Amanda died, killing her happily at the end of every verse, too young to understand the horror. Maybe it really was how she would have wanted to go.

If you see Amanda Palmer on the street, kill her, said the graffiti under the bridge in Boston. And beneath that somebody else wrote, That way she'll live forever.

We had blackberry jam and scones for tea. Asya said we should go up to the ballroom and pretend we were at a grand ball with gowns and invitations and ambassadors but Chloe said please no and she just wanted to go for a walk by the lake.

So we did.

At first we thought it was a swan or perhaps a dress that had blown off the clothes-line and into the water. We saw the white.

"It's a lady," said Chloe. She is the oldest of us, and says this means she has the sharpest eyes.

We thought she was alive. I mean, I did. I thought she was thinking. Asya said she thought she was alive too. Chloe said she knew she was dead all along.

We walked out a little way and pushed her back to the shore with sticks, like a toy boat.

I said, "It's Miss Palmer."

Asya said that the strains of being a governess must have got to her, with all the French and grammar and everything, and she expected that Miss Palmer had succumbed to brain fever.

Chloe didn't say anything at all. Not then.

The bruises on Miss Palmer's neck were the colour of blackberry jam.

Then we went up the hill to the house to tell people what we had found.

When we were waiting to tell them, Chloe said she saw Miss Palmer kissing someone in the scullery, two nights ago. Asya and I asked her who it was, but she said she did not know the gentleman, and only caught a glimpse.

We all agreed that a governess who died for love is a most romantic thing; but who will teach us pianoforte and sewing and composition now?

We had poached eggs for supper and then to bed. Asya and I listened to Chloe crying quietly in her bed, and eventually she stopped crying, and then we slept.

In the morning Miss Palmer was no longer to be seen, and Mama said the matter was not to be mentioned again. For tea we had gooseberry jam and toast.

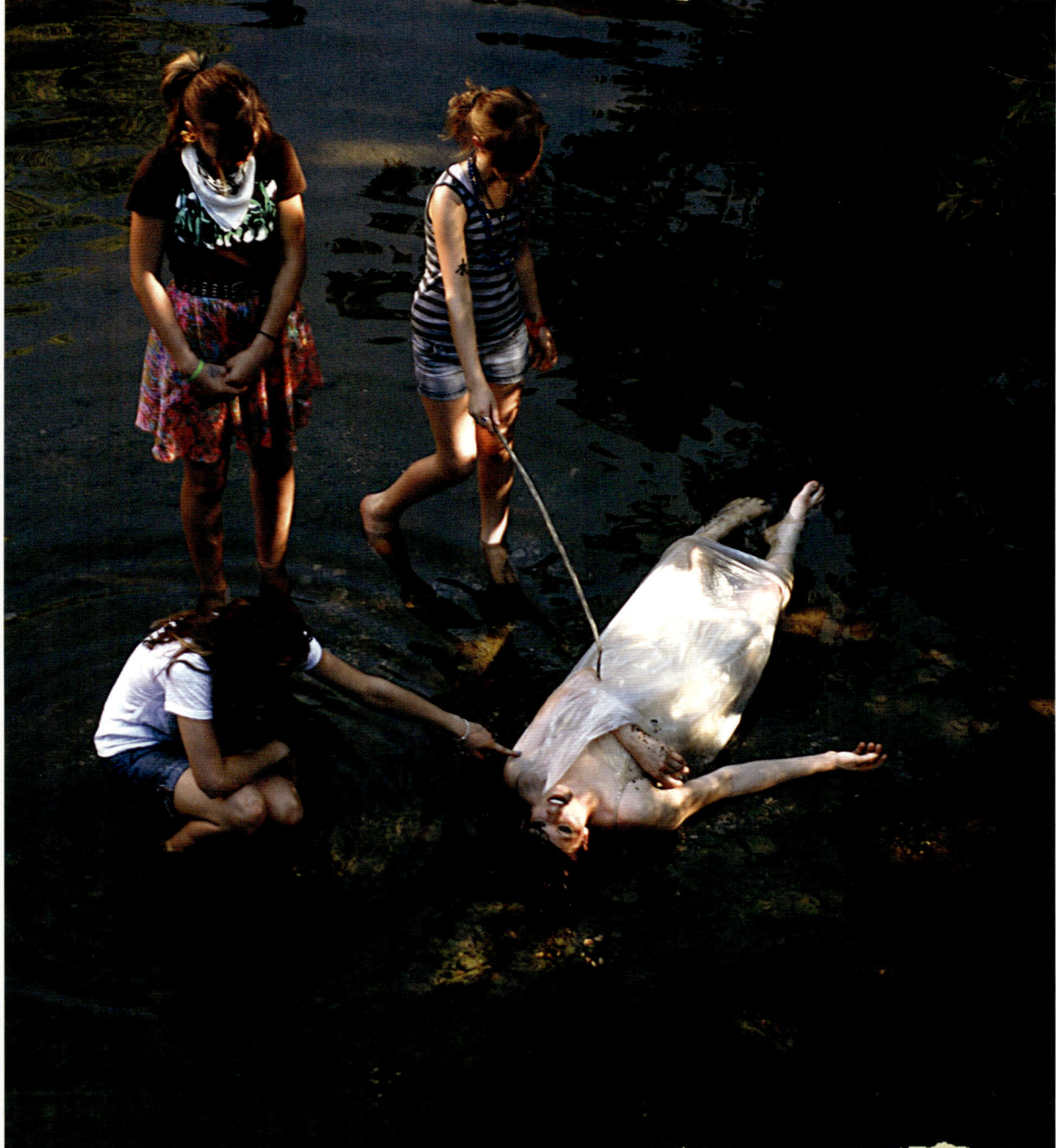

from the Private Diary of Maia Carlisle

ASTRONAUT

A short history of nearly nothing

is it enough to have some love
small enough to slip inside a book
small enough to cover with your hand
because everyone around you wants to look

is it enough to have some love
small enough to fit inside the cracks
the pieces don't fit together so good
with all the breaking and all the gluing back

and i am still not getting what i want
i want to touch the back of your right arm
i wish you could remind me who i was
because every day i'm a little further off

but you are, my love, the astronaut
flying in the face of science
i will gladly stay an afterthought
just bring back some nice reminders

and is it getting harder to pretend
that life goes on without you in the wake
and can you see the means without the end
in the random frantic action that we take

and is it getting easy not to care
despite the many rings around your name
it isn't funny and it isn't fair
you've traveled all this way and it's the same

but you are, my love, the astronaut
flying in the face of science
i will gladly stay an afterthought
just bring back some nice reminders

i would tell them anything to see you split the evening
but as you see i do not have an awful lot to tell
everybody's sick for something that they can find fascinating
everyone but you and even you aren't feeling well

but you are, my love, the astronaut
flying in the face of science
i will gladly stay an afterthought
just bring back some nice reminders

YES you are, my love, the astronaut
crashing in the name of science
just my luck they found your upper half
it's a very nice reminder
it's a very nice reminder

(and you may be acquainted with the night
but i have seen the darkness in the day
and you must know it is a terrifying sight
because you and i are living the same way)

We dine together every night.
Facing each other across the dinner table.
I painted her eyes on myself.

The closed eyes disturbed me.
I worried she was bored or asleep.
We dine together every night.

I talk to her about the world.
Not "Pass the salt." She does not pass anything.
I painted her eyes on myself.

The last time she spoke it was to complain about
  the food:
It was too bitter, and she disliked the mushrooms.
We dine together every night.

That was long ago. She no longer ages.
Between meals I keep her covered with a sheet.
We dine together every night.

I painted her eyes on myself.

AMANDA PALMER

RUNS IN THE FAMILY

my friend has problems with winter and autumn
they give him prescriptions, they shine bright lights on him
they say it's genetic, they say he can't help it
they say you can catch it—but sometimes you're born with it

my friend has blight he gets shakes in the night
and they say there is no way that they could have caught it in
time takes its toll on him, it is traditional
it is inherited predisposition

all day i've been wondering what is inside of me, who can i
blame for it

i say:

it runs in the family, this famine that carries me
to such great lengths to open my legs
up to anyone who'll have me
it runs in the family, i come by it honestly
do what you want 'cause who knows it might fill me up

my friend's depressed, she's a wreck, she's a mess
they've done all sorts of tests and they guess it has something
to do with her grandmother's
grandfather's grandmother civil war soldiers who
badly infected her
my friend has maladies, rickets, and allergies that she dates
back to the 17th century
somehow she manages—in her misery—strips in the city
and shares all her best tricks with

me? well, i'm well. well, i mean i'm in hell. well, i still
have my health
(at least that's what they tell me)
if wellness is this, what in hell's name is sickness?
but business is business!

and business
runs in the family, we tend to bruise easily
bad in the blood i'm telling you 'cause
i just want you to know me
know me and my family
we're wonderful folks but
don't get too close to me 'cause you might knock me up

mary have mercy now look what i've done
but don't blame me because i can't tell where i come from
and running is something that we've always done
well and mostly i can't even tell what i'm running from

i run from their pity
from responsibility
run from the country
and run from the city

i can run from the law
i can run from myself
i can run for my life
i can run into debt

i can run from it all

i can run till i'm gone
i can run for the office
and run from the 'cause

i can run using every last ounce of energy
i cannot
i cannot
i cannot
run from my family
they're hiding inside me
corpses on ice
come in if you'd like
but just don't tell my family
they'd never forgive me
they'll say that i'm crazy
but they would say anything if it would
shut me up. . . .

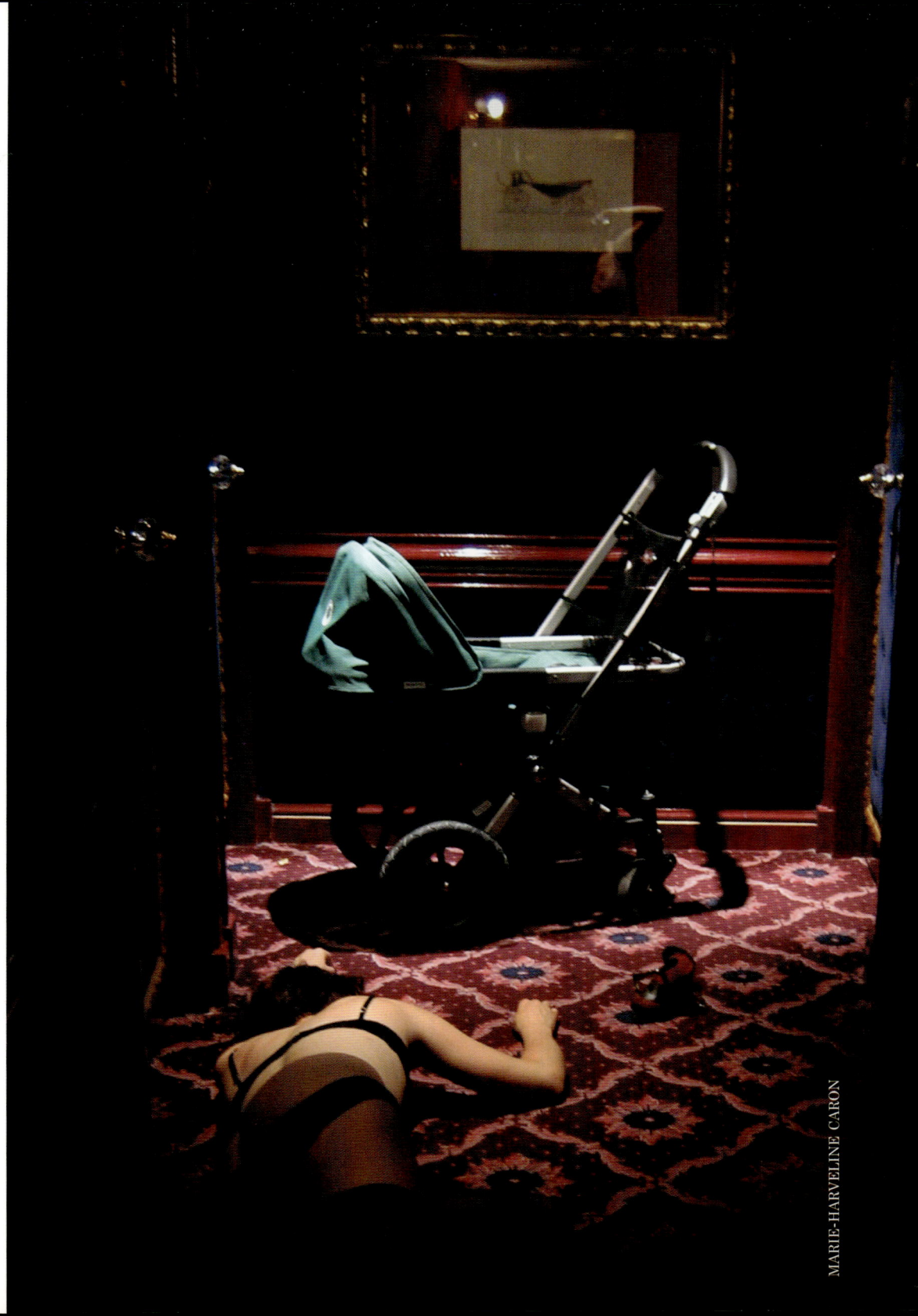

She said, but you never do anything.

He said, I do.

The hot air balloon drifted serenely above the world.

He fed another sheet of paper into the typewriter.

And that's another thing, she said. Nobody uses typewriters any more. They use computers. You could get a solar powered computer.

You cannot write a novel on a computer, he told her. Or at least, you cannot write this novel. He pointed to the manuscript on the floor of the balloon, beside the chicken-cage and the bucket and the cardboard boxes filled with clothes.

You cannot write a novel on a computer, she agreed. Then, you cannot do anything.

Don't say that, he said.

He typed the words THE END. Pulled the paper from the platen with a click and a ding. There, he told her. The novel. Five hundred pages. See? It's done. Wasn't that worth travelling the world in a hot air balloon?

No, she said.

He said nothing. He picked up the rock that weighed down the novel and placed the final sheet of paper beneath it. For a moment she wondered if he was going to hit her with the rock, was almost excited by the idea, but no. Emboldened, she continued.

It's not important because nothing you do is important. Even if your novel gets published, even if it gets read, it will change nothing. Nobody will live who would not have lived. Nothing will change. Can you imagine someone dying because of your words? I can't.

He picked up the Underwood typewriter and dropped it over the side of the balloon.

Do you think that changed anything for anyone, she asked. Changed anything?

It was like punching in a dream. He couldn't do anything, not even now.

No, he admitted.

No, she said, more tenderly.

They held hands as the balloon drifted slowly eastward. He missed his typewriter, but it was perfectly peaceful up there.

At the Crime Scene—
AMANDA PALMER

Fallen groceries
- Cans of soup
- (Laundry soap?)
- Typewriter

POSSIBILITIES—

- Freak weather (check for tornados)
- Orbital debris (no signs of
  burning or re-entry damage
  on typewriter)
- The hand of God ???

KYLE CASSIDY

NEMA, AGE 10 = 1
AFP = 0

OASIS

when i got to the party they gave me a forty
and i must have been thirsty
'cause i drank it so quickly
when i got to the bedroom
there was somebody waiting
and it isn't my fault that the barbarian raped me

when i went to get tested i brought along my best friend
melissa mahoney (who had once been molested)
and she knew how to get there
she knew all the nurses; they were all really friendly
but the test came out positive

i've had better days but i don't care
'cause i just sent a letter in the mail

when i got my abortion i brought along my boyfriend
we got there an hour before the appointment
and outside the building were all these annoying
fundamentalist christians; we tried to ignore them

i've had better days but i don't care
oasis got my letter in the mail

when vacation was over
the word was all over that i was a crackwhore
melissa had told them
and so now we're not talking except we have tickets
to see blur in october and i think we're still going

i've seen better days but i don't care
oh, i just got a letter in the mail
oasis sent a photograph it's autographed and everything
melissa's gonna wet herself i swear

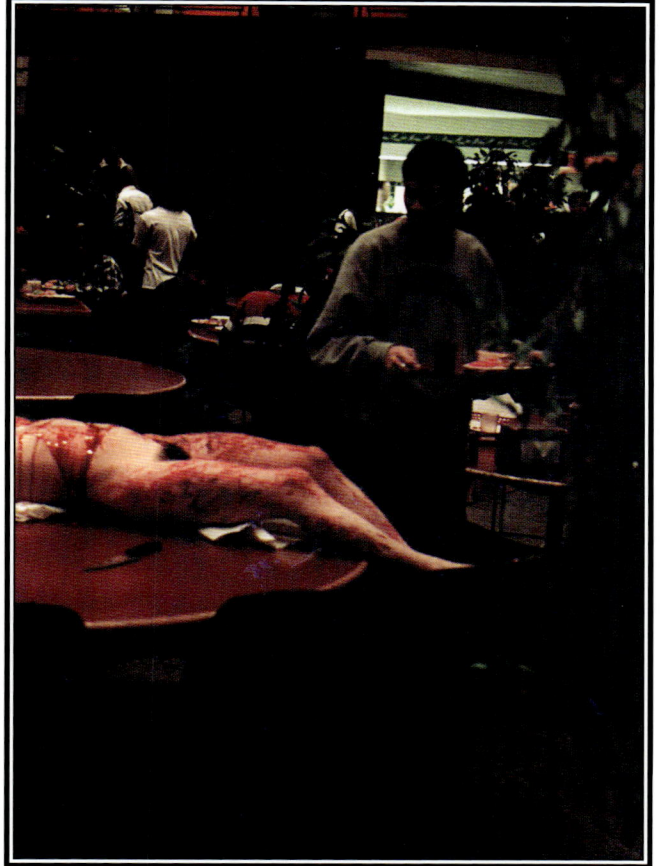

Following The Unfortunate Incident of the Award-Winning Turkey Hash, Miss Palmer's Breakfast Associates Plan Their Exit Strategy.

KYLE CASSIDY

JUN '73

THE SWORD

You only get to kill yourself once. Most people don't even get that. Amanda Palmer materialised in the alley in a crackle of blue sparks and the sharp scent of ozone, like all terminators. She had a sense of style, and you had to do these things properly.

She saw Amanda Palmer where she expected to see her, outside the nightclub's service entrance. She had stolen a moment for a cigarette, and was pulling at it angrily.

"Hi," Amanda said. "Want to come for a walk?"

Her younger self barely looked at her. "Leave me alone," she said. "It's been a long night."

"Come on," said Amanda. "You'll only have to go back in when you finish the cigarette. And you need the walk."

Amanda actually looked at her this time. She said, "You look calmer than I feel."

"Time," said Amanda. "It's not as scary as you think it is."

"If it's not scary," said Amanda, padding by her side through the streets of Boston, "then what are the swords for?"

"They are to make it fair."

She said it, and knew as she said it that it would not be fair. It wasn't. The younger Amanda had youth and speed on her side, but Amanda had craft and cunning and experience; she had learned to be bloodthirsty.

Amanda had thought it would be a hard thing, killing her younger self, but, at the end, she found it easy, almost pleasant, to administer the killing stroke.

She had hoped that Amanda would ask her why. She even had a speech prepared, all about art and compromise. It was a fucken kick-ass speech and she was disappointed not to have been able to deliver it.

And then there was an ozone crackle and she was home.

—How was it?
—Oddly satisfying, she said.

She cleaned the blood from the blade, rubbed it with mineral oil, hung it back on the wall above her door.

—You won?

—Well, I'd been practicing. I guess I don't need to practice any longer.

—No?

A pause, and then,

—What happens if a you from the future arrives here?

—That isn't going to happen. Not ever. I'm not going to fucken compromise.

Silence.

She reached up to the wall above the door, pulled down the sword, commenced to parry, to thrust, to fight shadows.

Once upon the olden times, when the trees walked and the stars danced, there was a girl whose mother died, and a new mother came and married her father, bringing her own daughter with her. Soon enough the father followed his first wife to the grave, leaving his daughter behind him.

The new mother did not like the girl and treated her badly, always favouring her own daughter, who was indolent and rude. One day, her stepmother gave the girl, who was only eighteen, twenty dollars to buy her drugs. "Don't stop on the way," she said.

So the girl took the twenty dollar bill, and put an apple into her purse, for the way was long, and she walked out of the house and down to the end of the street, where the wrong side of town began.

She saw a dog tied to a lamppost, panting and uncomfortable in the heat, and the girl said, "Poor thing." She gave it water.

The elevator was out of service. The elevator there was always out of service. Half way up the stairs she saw a hooker, with a swollen face, who stared up at her with yellow eyes. "Here," said the girl. She gave the hooker the apple.

She went up to the dealer's floor and she knocked on the door three times. The dealer opened the door and stared at her and said nothing. She showed him the twenty dollar bill.

Then she said, "Look at the state of this place," and she bustled in. "Don't you ever clean up in here? Where are your cleaning supplies?"

The dealer shrugged. Then he pointed to a closet. The girl opened it and found a broom and a rag. She filled the bathroom sink with water and she began to clean the place.

When the rooms were cleaner, the girl said, "Give me the stuff for my stepmother."

He went into the bedroom, came back with a plastic bag.

The girl pocketed the bag and walked down the stairs.

"Lady," said the hooker. "The apple was good. But I'm hurting real bad. You got anything?"

The girl said, "It's for my stepmother."

"Please?"

"You poor thing."

The girl hesitated, then she gave her the packet. "I'm sure my stepmother will understand," she said.

She left the building. As she passed, the dog said, "You shine like a diamond, girl."

She got home. Her mother was waiting in the front room. "Where is it?" she demanded.

"I'm sorry," said the girl. Diamonds dropped from her lips, rattled across the floor.

Her stepmother hit her.

"Ow!" said the girl, a ruby red cry of pain, and a ruby fell from her lips.

Her stepmother fell to her knees, picked up the jewels. "Pretty," she said. "Did you steal them?"

The girl shook her head, scared to speak.

"Do you have any more in there?"

The girl shook her head, mouth tightly closed.

The stepmother took the girl's tender arm between her finger and her thumb and pinched as hard as she could, squeezed until the tears glistened in the girl's eyes, but she said nothing. So her stepmother locked the girl in her windowless bedroom, so she could not get away.

The woman took the diamonds and the ruby to Al's Pawn and Gun, on the corner, where Al gave her five hundred dollars no questions asked.

Then she sent her other daughter off to buy drugs for her.

The girl was selfish. She saw the dog panting in the sun, and, once she was certain that it was chained up and could not follow, she kicked at it. She pushed past the hooker on the stair.

She reached the dealer's apartment and knocked on the door. He looked at her, and she handed him the twenty without speaking. On her way back down, the hooker on the stair said, "Please...?" but the girl did not even slow.

"Bitch!" called the hooker.

"Snake," said the dog, when she passed it on the sidewalk.

Back home, the girl took out the drugs, then opened her mouth to say "Here," to her mother. A small frog, brightly coloured, slipped from her lips. It leapt from her arm to the wall, where it hung and stared at them unblinking.

"Oh my god," said the girl. "That's just disgusting." Five more coloured tree frogs, and one small red, black and yellow banded snake.

"Black against red," said the girl. "Is that poisonous?" (Three more tree frogs, a cane toad, a small, blind white snake, and a baby iguana.) She backed away from them.

Her mother, who was not afraid of snakes or of anything, kicked at the banded snake, which bit her leg. The woman screamed and flailed, and her daughter also began to scream, a long loud scream which fell from her lips as a healthy adult python.

The girl, the first girl, whose name was Amanda, heard the screams and then the silence but she could do nothing to find out what was happening.

She knocked on the door. No one opened it. No one said anything. The only sounds she could hear were rustlings, as if of something huge and legless slipping across the carper.

When Amanda got hungry, too hungry for words, she began to speak.

"Thou still unravish'd bride of quietness," she began. "Thou foster child of Silence and slow time..."

She spoke, although the words were choking her.

"Beauty is truth, truth beauty – that is all ye know on Earth, and all ye need to know..." A final sapphire clicked across the wooden floor of Amanda's closet.

The silence was absolute.

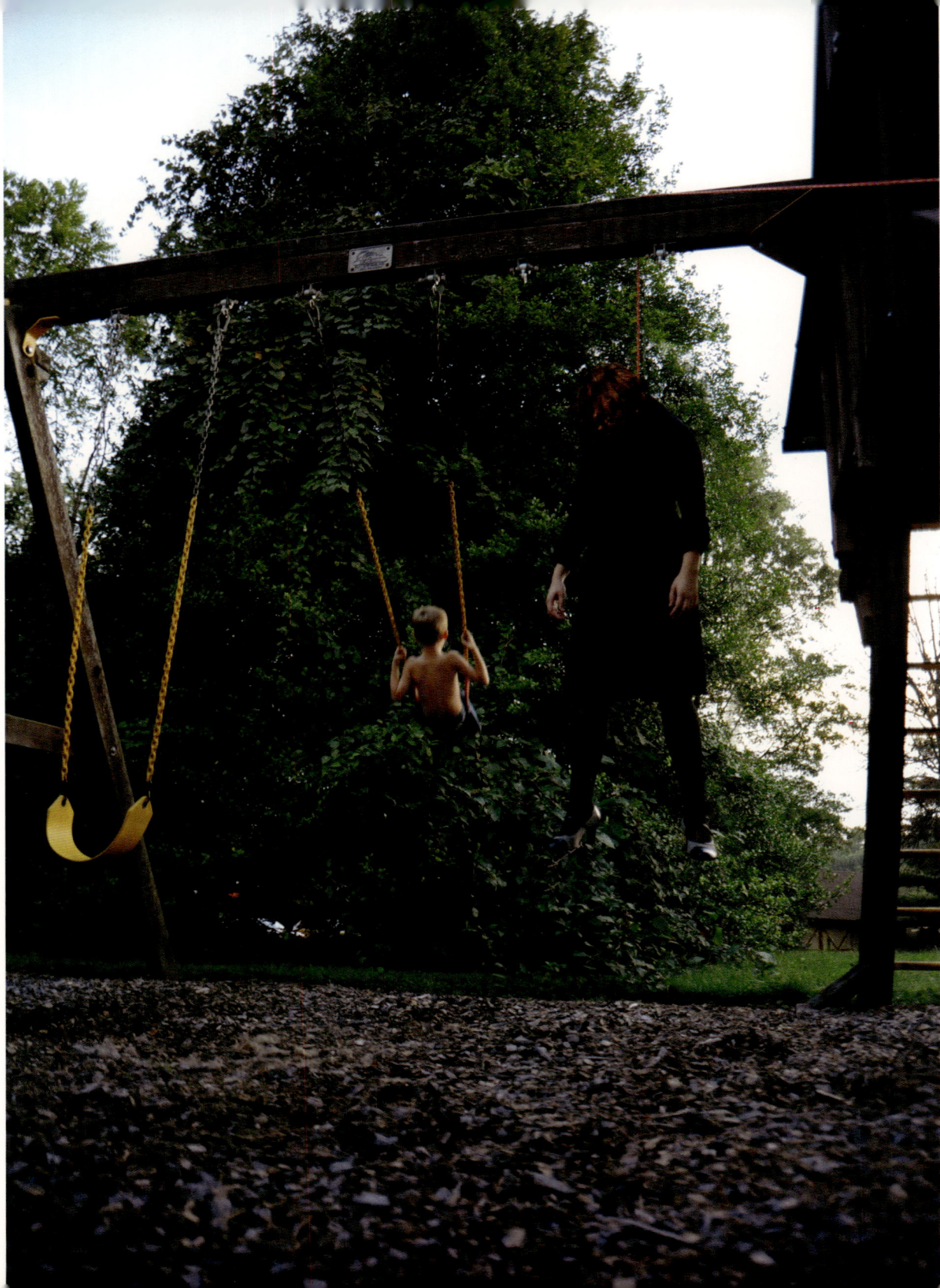

BLAKE SAYS

blake says no one ever really loved him
they just faked it to get money from the government
and blake thinks angels grow when you plant angel dust
he shakes his head and blinks his pretty eyes but trust me
he's no valentine though he said he would be mine
his heart is in alaska all the time

blake stays underwater for the most part
he collects loose change for all tomorrow's parties
and when blake dates girls with tattoos of the pyramids
he breaks their hearts by saying it's not permanent
but in his velvet mind he believes with all his might
we'll all go to alaska when we die . . .

blake makes friends but only for a minute
he prefers the things he orders from the internet
and blake's been having trouble with his head again
he takes his pills but never takes his medicine
he tells me that he's fine
and the sad thing is he's right
and when its 2 o'clock it feels like 9 . . .

blake says he is sorry he got through to me
if it's ok he'll call right back and talk to the machine
blake says it looks like acid rain today
he takes the fish inside, he's very kind that way
and just like caroline
he doesn't seem to mind
the globe is getting warmer all the time . . .

it's still cold in alaska
it's still cold in alaska
it's still cold in alaska

THE INTERNATIONAL
AMUSEMENT
COMPANY

FIRE

regina kays they're just old light

THE PASSION OF ST. AMANDA

THE GIRL IN THE CARPET

THE TWO OF THEM

I have a presentiment of doom," said one of the Palmer twins.

"Do you, dear," said the other, her older by several minutes.

"I do. I am convinced that something terrible is going to happen."

"But it's such a beautiful day." She stirred her tea. Then, "Did you hear that?"

"What?"

"I think it was footsteps."

The first twin shivered. "I heard nothing," she said. "And yet . . . my bedroom was disturbed when I went up there this morning. Things had been moved. My jewelry case was out."

"Had anything been taken?"

"Not a thing. And I saw a shadow in the garden. Did I tell you that?"

"What was it the shadow of?"

"It was just a shadow."

"Nonsense, dear. It doesn't work like that. You don't have a shadow if you don't have something casting the shadow."

Her twin appeared unconvinced.

The older of the Palmer twins sipped her tea, hot and strong, just as she liked it.

A noise in the hallway. She leaned around to see.

"I am certain that I heard footsteps that time," she said. "Do not tell me you did not hear them." She waited for her twin to respond, to say anything, absolutely anything, anything at all.

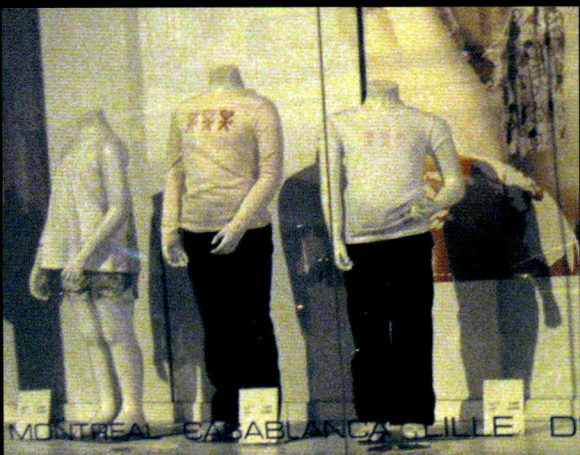

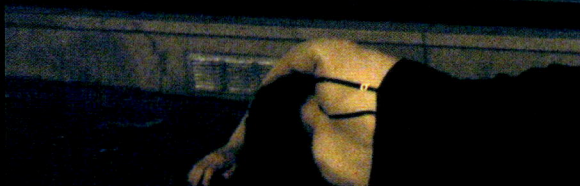

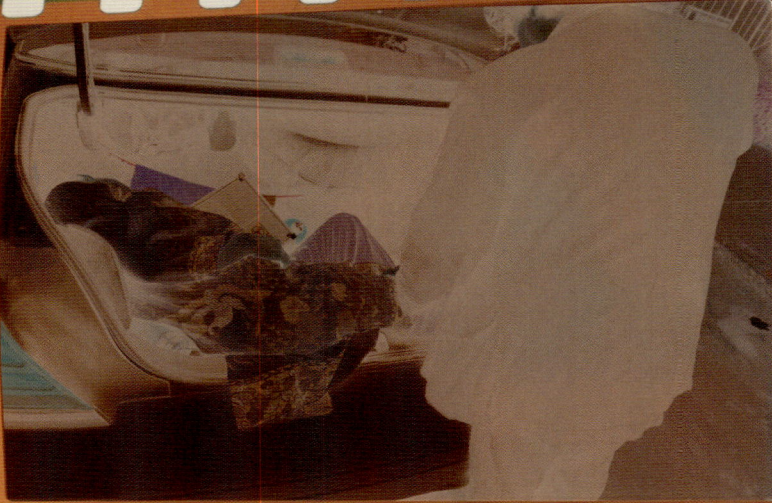

HAVE TO DRIVE

i have to drive
i have my reasons, deer
it's cold outside
i hate the seasons here

i suffer mornings most of all
i feel so powerless and small
by 10 o'clock i'm back in bed
fighting the jury in my head

we learn to drive
it's only natural, deer
we drive all night
we haven't slept in years

we suffer mornings most of all
we saw you lying in the road
we tried to dig a decent grave
but it's still no way to behave

it is a delicate position
spin the bottle
pick the victim

catch a tiger
switch directions
if he hollers
break his ankles
to protect him

we'll have to drive
they're getting closer
just get inside
it's almost over

we will save your brothers we
will save your cousins we will drive them
far away from streets and lights
from all signs of mad mankind

we suffer mornings most of all
wake up all bleary-eyed and sore
forgetting everything we saw

i'll meet you in an hour
at the car.

CAT FOOD

AMPERSAND

i walk down my street at night
the city lights are cold and violent
i am comforted by the approaching sound of trucks and sirens
even though the world's so bad, these men rush out to help the dying
and though i am no use to them i do my part by simply smiling

the ghetto boys are cat-calling me
as i pull my keys from my pocket
i wonder if this method of courtship has ever been effective
has any girl in history said "sure, you seem so nice, let's get it on"
still i always shock them when i answer "hi, my name's amanda" and

i'm not gonna live my life
on one side of an ampersand
and even if i went with you
i'm not the girl you think i am
and i'm not gonna match you
'cause i'll lose my voice completely
no, i'm not gonna watch you
'cause i'm not the one that's crazy

i have wasted years of my life
agonizing about the fires
i started when i thought that to be strong you must be flame-retardant
and now to dress the wounds calls into question
how authentic they are
there is always someone criticizing me
she just likes playing hospital

lying in my bed
i remember what you said
"there's no such thing as accidents . . ."

but you've got the headstones all ready
all carved up and pretty
your sick satisfaction
those his and hers matching

the daisies all push up in pairs to the horizon
your eyes full of ketchup, it's nice that you're trying
the headstones all ready
all carved up and pretty
your sick satisfaction
those his and hers matching
the daisies all push up in pairs to the horizon
your eyes full of ketchup, it's nice that you're trying

but i'm not gonna live my life
on one side of an ampersand
and even if i went with you
i'm not the girl you think i am

and i'm not gonna match you
'cause i'll lose my voice completely
no, i'm not gonna watch you
'cause i'm not the one that's crazy

as i wake up—two o'clock—the fire burned the block but ironically
stopped at my apartment and my housemates are all sleeping soundly
and nobody deserves to die, but you were awful adamant
that if i didn't love you then you had just one alternative
and i may be romantic
and i may risk my life for it
but i ain't gonna die for you
you know i ain't no juliet
and i'm not gonna watch you
while you burn yourself out, baby
no, i'm not gonna stop you
'cause i'm not the one that's crazy

Anonymous Artist
November 10

who killed amanda palmer   **$672,000**
installation. sofa. leaves. amanda palmer (dead). plasterboard. paint.

In its time this installation was considered remarkable for its use of a fresh human body obtained, according to the anonymous artist, perfectly legitimately. The casing is nearly airtight. The piece reinterprets the literality of its title by the artist's own anonymity and refusal to discuss the work – to provide answers to the question (or, more precisely, the statement) that forms its title. The artist declines to explain how she obtains a fresh human body in each place the work has been exhibited.

In Madrid in 1998 the body was omitted. In all other locations the model was installed at the beginning of the exhibition, and natural decay was permitted to take its course. The Nantes, Edinburgh, Warsaw and Boston installations are all able to be viewed in time-lapse photography, now as Quicktime films on the web.

According to the anonymous artist, the decay of the body represents the loss of joy in the world; the leaves are innocence; the sofa may be seen as representing hope, desire, or the breakdown of the capitalist system. The flies, which may gather in increasing numbers in the latter weeks of the exhibit, should be viewed as part of the installation.

CHRISTIE'S
NEW YORK

IGNORANZA.

FVRORE.

FALSITA D'AMORE.

MANGIA BENE.

TVRCO.

SVPERBIA.

MODERN LOVE

Dear Amanda,

Or can I call you, not dear, but dearest. Because you are. You are my dearest, most precious, most marvelous dear. At night I dream of you and in the morning I wake with your name on my lips. Truly—I wake, and say your name. Is that not ridiculous? But do not ridicule me. I am, after all, a man in love.

Marry me.

There, I have said it. I want to look at you always, to look up and see the tilt of your smile, the slight crook of your teeth, the paint-splash blue of your eyes. I want your kiss and your embrace. And in return I will keep you safe.

Nothing will harm you, if you marry me. I will spend my days plotting ways to make your life more pleasant. I shall bring you little gifts and flowers—not a day will dawn without flowers. And your welfare will be more important to me than my own. Every word you utter will be as an order to me. Your tiniest whim will be my command.

And all I would ask in return is your love. Your hand in marriage. I want you to bear my children, want you to prepare my meals and clean my house, you and you only to make our bed each morning and you to be there for me, at the end of the day, with a smile on your face, as I return from a hard day's work.

I exaggerate of course. Should you wish a career outside the home I would support you in this, as in everything. And yet, something tells me that you would not need this to be happy. I will make your world modern in every way.

We will make a stylish couple, my dearest. We shall be the couple that the other newlyweds on our street will envy.

You will want for nothing.

Please say yes, and make me the happiest man in the world—and yourself the happiest woman.

I am yours,

and only yours,

Till Death us do part . . .

THE BOYS ROOM

He said, Hey I got to talk to you. It's about Amanda. She came over last night.

We got kinda stupid. I guess she said some dumb stuff. We both did.

And now we're not talking.

Well, she's not talking.

I guess maybe you oughtta come up and see for yourself.

STRENGTH THROUGH MUSIC

locked in his bedroom
he saw the world
a web of answers
and cumshot girls

tick tick tick tick tick

don't bother blaming
his games and guns
he's only playing
and boys just want to have fun

he picked a soundtrack
and packed his bag
he hung his walkman
around his neck

tick tick tick tick tick
tick tick tick tick tick

it is so simple
the way they fall
no bang or whimper
no sound at all

tick tick tick tick tick
tick tick tick tick tick
tick tick tick tick tick tick tick tick tick

boom.

GUITAR HERO

i can't get them up, i can't get them up
i can't get them up at all

(hey. ho. let. go.)

good morning killer king you're a star
that's gorgeous hold it right where you are
the weather's kinda lousy today
so what oh what oh what'll we play

stratocaster strapped to your back
it's a semi-automatic like dad's
he taught you how to pause and reset
and that's about as far as you get

so what's the use of going outside?
it's so depressing when people die in real life
i'd rather pick up right where we left
making out to faces of death
making out to faces of death

and i could save you, baby, but it isn't worth my time
and i could make you chase me for a little price is right

it's a hit but are you actually sure?
the targets in the crowd are a blur
the people screaming just like they should
but you don't even know if you're good
you don't even know if you're good

so tie them up and feed them the sand
ha nigga! try hard to tell us using your hands
a picture's worth a million words
and that way nobody gets hurt
and that way nobody gets hurt

and i could save you, baby, but it isn't worth my time
and i could make you chase me for a little price is right

woo-ah-oo - woo-ooh-ah-oo
woo-ah-ooh ah ohh ah oo

you're my guitar hero, you're my guitar hero
you're my guitar hero, you're my guitar hero

x marks the box in the hole in the ground that goes off at a breath
so careful don't make a sound
x marks the box in the hole in your head that you dug for yourself
now lie. in. it.

shut up about all of that negative shit
you wanted to make it and now that you're in
you're obviously not gonna die
so why not take your chances and try
why not take your chances and try?

how do you get them to turn this thing off?
this isn't at all like the ones back at home
just shut your eyes and flip the cassette
and that's about the time that they hit
and that's about the time that they hit

what the fuck is up with this shit?
it's certainly not worth getting upset
his hands are gone and most of his head
and just when he was getting so good
just when he was getting so good . . .

and i could save you, baby, but it isn't worth my time
'cause even if i saved you there's a million more in line

woo-ah-oo - woo-ooh-ah-oo
woo-ah-ooh ah ohh ah oo

you're my guitar hero, you're my guitar hero
you're my guitar hero
you're my guitar hero

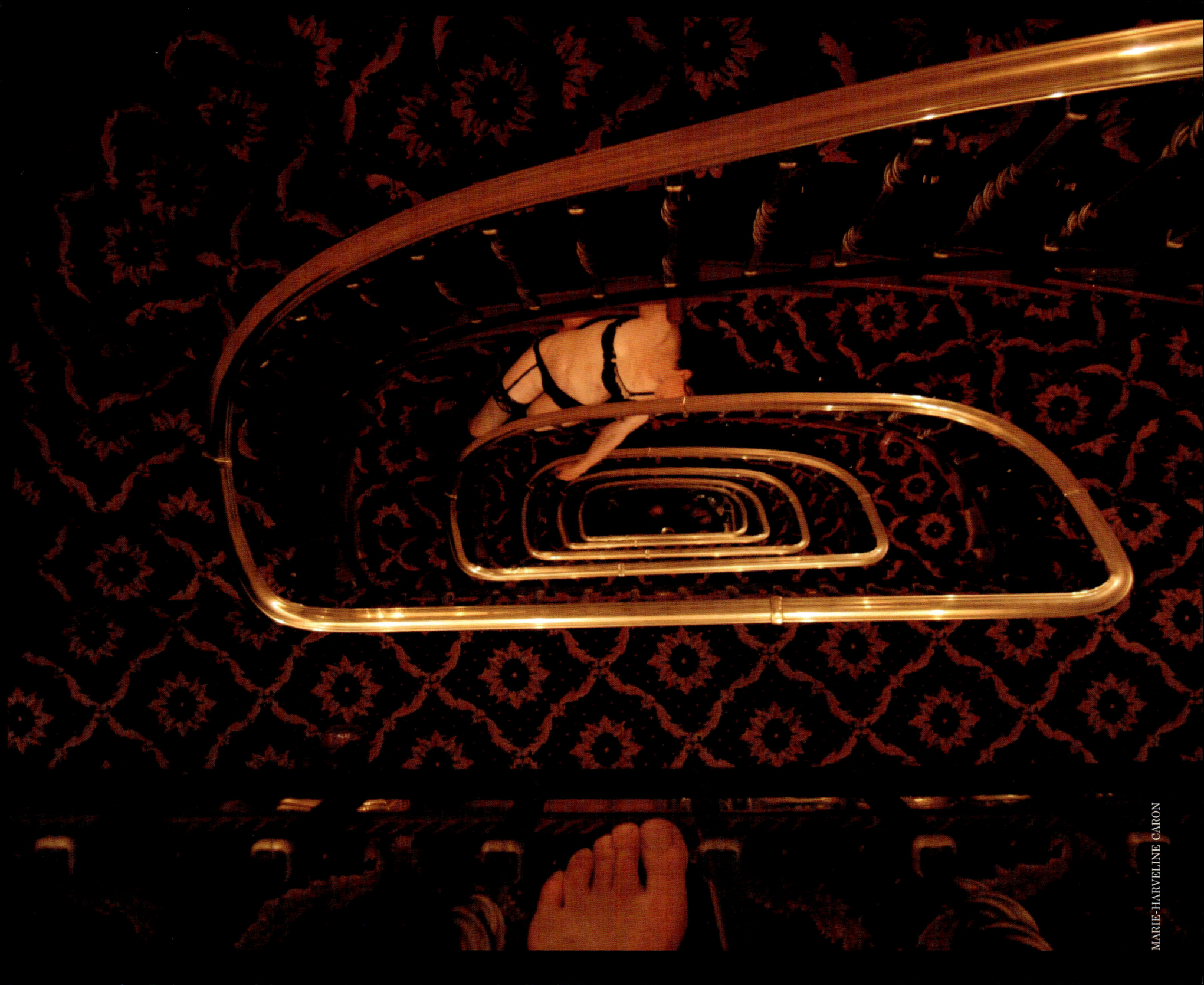

LEEDS UNITED

we watch you your expert double exes
it's just like you to paint those whiter fences

it's so polite it's so polite it's offensive it's offensive
it's so unright it's so unright it's a technical accept it

but who needs love when there's law & order
and who needs love when there's southern comfort
and who needs love at all

we stalk you your expert double exes
we oxidize you in your sleep there's no exit there's no exit

you're on a roll you're on a roll no one gets it no one gets it
your honor no your honor can't you protect us, protect us

but who needs love when there's law & order
and who needs love when there's southern comfort
and who needs love
when the sandwiches are wicked and they know you at the mac store

uh uh uh uh oh oh oh oh oh uh oh - i'm so excited
uh uh uh uh oh oh oh oh oh uh oh - the blacks and beat kids
uh uh uh uh oh oh oh oh oh uh oh - i'm getting frightened
uh uh uh uh uh uh uh uh - someday someday leeds united

bugsy malone came to carry you home and they're taking you all to the doctor
burberry vices all sugary spices it's nice but it's not what i'm after

sure, i admire you
sure, you inspire me but you've been not getting back so
i'll wait at the sainbury's countin' my change making BANK on the
upcoming roster

and we'll stop you your expert double exes
oh yeah, a big stock holder exxtra cold with 2 X's
that never talking thing you do is effective it's effective
your shoulder's icy colder-oh than a death wish than a death wish

but who needs love when there's law & order
and who needs love when there's dukes of hazzard
and who needs love
when the sandwiches are wicked and they know you at the mac store

uh uh uh uh oh oh oh oh oh uh oh - i'm so excited
uh uh uh uh oh oh oh oh oh uh oh - the blacks and beat kids
uh uh uh uh oh oh oh oh oh uh oh - they're so excited
uh uh uh uh oh oh oh oh oh uh oh - when i think about leeds uniting
uh uh uh uh oh oh oh oh oh uh oh - i'm getting frightened
uh uh uh uh oh oh oh oh oh uh oh - the blacks, the blacks, the blacks, and
beat kids
uh uh uh uh oh oh oh oh oh uh oh - it's so exciting
uh uh uh uh oh oh oh oh oh uh oh - someday, someday, someday,
someday, someday, someday

LEEDS UNITED.

THE CASE OF THE BESMIRCHED DIRNDL

I will advise the police," said the consulting detective, "that they are looking for a man. He is dark-haired, left-handed, and extremely tall, in all probability a basketball player. He has spent time in Bavaria, but his passport is almost definitely Guatamalan. He was here for the woodwind convention, but will have checked out early."

"Good heavens," I told him. "How on earth . . . ?"

"You know my methods," said my friend. "Apply them."

THE POINT OF IT ALL

oh, what a noble, distinguished collection of fine little friends you have made
hitting the tables without you again: no we'll wait, no we promise, we'll wait
june makes these excellent sewing machines out of common industrial waste
she spends a few months at a time on the couch but she's safe
she wears shades, she wears shades

but no one can stare at the wall as good as you, my babydoll
and you're aces for coming along
you're almost human, after all
and you're learning that just 'cause they call themselves friends
doesn't mean they'll call . . .

they made the comment in jest
but you've got the needle
i guess that's the point of it all

maybe a week in the tropics would help to remind you how nice life can be
we propped you right up in a chair on a deck with a beautiful view of the sea
but a couple weeks later we came back and you and the chair were nowhere
to be seen
you had magically moved to the closet
eyes fixed to the place where the dryer had been

oh, but no one can stare at the wall as good as you, my babydoll
and you're aces for coming along
you're almost human, after all
why on earth would i keep you propped up in here when you so love the fall . . . ?

the pattern's laid out on the bed
with dozens of colors of thread
but you've got the needle
i guess that's the point in the end

but it's better to waste your day watching the scenery change at a comatose rate
than to put yourself in it and turn into one of those cigarette ads that you hate
but while you were sleeping some men came around
said they had some dimensions to take
i'm not sure what they were talking about but they sure made a mess of your face

but still, no one can stare at the wall as good as you, my babydoll
and you're aces for playing along
you're almost human, even now

and just 'cause they call themselves experts
it doesn't mean sweet fuck all . . .
they've got the permanent press
homes with a stable address

and they've got excitement
and life by the fistful
but you've got the needle
i guess that's the point of it all

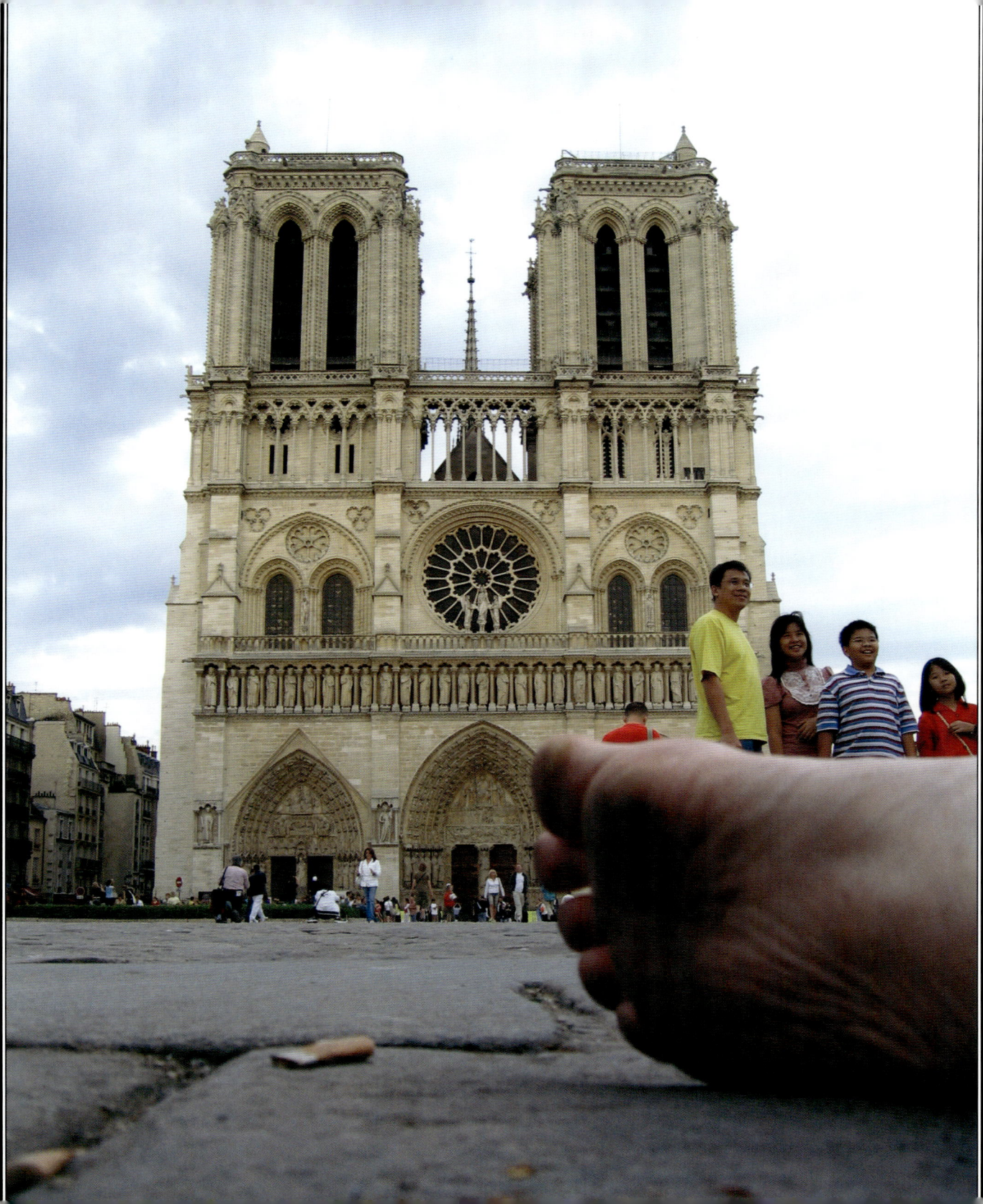

VEGAN

Louvre Museum (Paris, France)

Dear Miss B.

Having a wonderful time.

Wish you were her.

A friend

Miss Beatrice Zerrière
266 Van Buren St.
Brooklyn, NY
11221
USA

AMANDA PALMER

AMANDA PALMER

Singer and driver die
in rock tour crash

Nicola Berkovic

A MEMBER of a Victorian death
metal band was killed along with the
group's driver when their
car veered off a highway in
NSW yesterday and

ANOTHER YEAR

i tried to fall in it again
my friends took bets and disappeared
they mime their sighing violins
i think i'll wait another year

i want my chest pressed to your chest
my nervous systems interfere
ten or eleven months at best
i think i'll wait another year

this weather turns my tricks to rust
i am a lousy engineer
the winter makes things hard enough
i think i'll wait another year

plus, i'm only 26 years old
my grandma died at 83
that's lots of time if i don't smoke
i think i'll wait another year

i'm not as callous as you think
i barely breathe when you are near
it's not as bad when i don't drink
i think i'll wait another year

i have my new bill hicks cd
i have my friends and my career
i'm getting smaller by degrees
you said you'd help me disappear
but that could take forever
i think i'll wait another year
it'll be the best year ever
i think i'll wait another . . .

can't we just wait together?
you bring the smokes, i'll bring the beer

. . . i think i'll wait another year

MARIE-HARVELINE CARON

Amanda Palmer, the famous dancer, is dead in the only seat in the theatre. The seat is plastic. The original seats were removed years ago, disturbing the families of rats that nested in the horsehair and the springs, were hauled away and burned. The theatre was locked and forgotten years ago. It should be locked now.

Amanda Palmer, the eminent actress, is standing on the stage. She is invoking the Sun. She is waiting for the miracle that she was promised.

Clutched in the hand of the Amanda Palmer on the chair is a classified advertisement ripped from a newspaper, promising spiritual renewal. Her purse is missing. She may not be breathing.

On stage, Amanda hears her voice echoing back from the rear of the old theatre, the acoustics disturbingly sharp in that room with no seats. The smell of dust and mildew fills the cavernous auditorium. She has ovarian cancer. She also holds a newspaper clipping, the twin to the other Amanda's.

The roof of the theatre collapsed last year, and it is now open to the sky.

Amanda Palmer is waiting for the sunlight to fall on her face. Then she will close her eyes and let her face stare ecstatically upwards.

Amanda Palmer dropped the empty wine bottle when she stopped breathing. She can hear singing coming from the stage.

Amanda Palmer feels the sun on her face. She knows that the life-giving energy is even now renewing her cells, shrinking the tumours, making her whole. She swims inside herself, eyes closed, thinking of promises.

Promises contained in cheap wine, and in newspaper cuttings and in a voice on the other end of the telephone.

The Amanda on the chair hears nothing any longer, and is now beginning to grow cold. While on the stage Amanda Palmer tries to blink away the afterimages that blur her vision, and makes her exit from the stage, certain only that she is cured, that the voice that promised so much has spoken the truth. And in this, as in so much, she is wrong.

AMANDA PALMER would like to thank the incredibly talented photographers who created art for this book: Ben Cerf, Kyle Cassidy, Tom Dickins, Lauren Goldberg, Amandacera Hannon, Marie-Harveline Caron, Regis Hertrich, Beth Hommel, Ryan Krakowsky, Michael McQuilken, Gregory Nomoora, Ron Nordin, Oliver Orion, Tegan Rain, Malka Resnicoff, Nicholas Vargelis and Anabel Vázquez Rodríguez. Thanks also to those who make special appearances in this book: Jason Webley, Lyndon Chester, Steven Mitchell Wright, Tora Hylands, Katrina Cornwell, and Mark Hill; Chloe, Aysa and Maia of Smoosh; Edward Albee; Kira Kupfersberg; Brian Viglione; Michael McQuilken and Beth Hommel; Emily White and Regina Spektor; Max Melton; members of The Citizens Band; Anna Vogelzang, Emilyn Brodsky and Daniel Oestreich; Hayley Maged and the WeKAP participants. And thank you to everyone else who helped make these photographs and this book a reality: Lee Barron and the Cloud Club, BriAnna Olsen, Michael Pope, Noah Blumenson-Cook, Casey Long, James Holland, Lydia Berg-Hammond and Katrina Bleckley. Also due big thanks: Harvey Leeds, Harry and Sandy Choron, Beth Hommel and Emily White. Thanks to everyone on theshadowbox.net. . . . and a very, very special extra thanks to Ron Nordin, an amazing artist in his own right. He *helped* us pay for the printing of this book. Long *Live the Punk* Cabaret.

KYLE CASSIDY would like to thank Annaliese Moyer, Liana Olear, Joe Kubinski, Paula Montrie, John Montrie, Lyn Belzer-Tonnessen, Jeffrey Holmes, Jeff Poretsky, Gina Mai Denn, Parthena Kydes, Lauren Julien, Nathen Ezra Wurzel, Kevin Hollenbeck, Koob Choat, Diane Donaldson, Dave Choat, Maureen Shanahan, Aster Grahn, Brian Moors, Jeffery Holmes, Jeffery Poretsky, Marcia Litt, Morrigan Condo, Kelli Biggs, Greykell Dutton, Sarah Alysandra Dutton, Gina Mae Denn, John Cooper, Jay Donaldson/Donaldson Funeral Home of Laurel, MD. Trillian Stars, Mike Vanhelder, Jennifer Summerfield, Jerry Rudisill & Deva, JR Blackwell, Jared Axelrod. Lee at the Cloud Club. Ego Likeness, Nicole Blackman, Tom Purdom, Brainclaw. B.D., Sarah, & Nick Colen. Karen Mack, who gave me my first Sandman comic book and made sure I grew up cool. Oakes, Sawyer, Olivia, Heather & John Dobson. Super extra special thanks to Beth Hommel for Being There and doing All That.

NEIL GAIMAN is currently serving 25 years to life at Sing Sing Correctional Facility for killing Amanda Palmer.